The Chugger Championship

Adapted by Michael Anthony Steele
Based on the story by Claudia Silver and Sarah Ball

SCHOLASTIC INC.
New York   Toronto   London   Auckland
Sydney   Mexico City   New Delhi   Hong Kong

ISBN 978-0-545-23315-6

© September 2010
© Ludorum plc 2010. Chuggington® is a registered trademark of Ludorum plc.
All rights reserved. Published by Scholastic Inc.
SCHOLASTIC and associated logos are trademarks and/or registered
trademarks of Scholastic Inc.
12 11 10 9 8 7 6 5 4 3 2 1   10 11 12 13 14 15/0

Printed in the U.S.A.   40
First printing, September 2010

It was a beautiful day in Chuggington. The chuggers were gathered at the train depot for a big announcement.

"Good morning, chuggers," said Vee, the announcer. "Tomorrow is the Chugger Championship! It's a race around Chuggington. The winner gets a trophy!"

"Traintastic!" said Koko. "I'm really fast!"
"Come on," she said to her best friends,
Wilson and Brewster. "Let's go practice!"

Koko and Wilson lined up for a practice race.
"On your tracks . . . get set . . . go!" Brewster shouted.

Koko zoomed ahead. She was so excited to be in the lead that she turned down the wrong set of tracks.

"And Wilson wins by a headlight!" shouted Brewster.
"But I'm faster than you," said Koko. "I should have won!"
Wilson laughed. "I am the champion!" he sang.
"We'll see about that tomorrow," Koko said, storming away.

The next day, the chuggers gathered in the depot for the race.

Koko and Wilson lined up side by side without saying a word. They both wanted to win.

"On your tracks . . . get set . . . GO!" called Vee.

Old Puffer Pete was looking for a safe spot to watch the race. But when Koko zipped up behind him, he realized he was on the same track as the racers!

Hmm . . . thought Pete. "Maybe there's still
spark in this old engine!" he shouted.
He decided to join the race.

All over Chuggington, people cheered the chuggers as they raced. Wilson had an idea. "Look, Koko!" he shouted. "Someone wants to take your picture!"

Koko smiled and pulled to a stop. "That's because *I'm* the fastest!" she said.

"Can't catch me!" Wilson shouted as he sped by her. Koko had been tricked. "Hey, that's not fair!" she cried.

Koko got back on track and chugged down the rails. She caught up to Wilson who was stopped at a turn.

"Koko, help!" Wilson cried. "I went too fast and now I'm out of fuel!"

"Yeah, right," said Koko. "I'm not falling for your tricks again."

"It's not a trick," Wilson pleaded, but Koko had already passed him.

Suddenly, Wilson heard a train speeding toward him. It was Emery the rapid transport chugger.

Emery couldn't see Wilson beyond the turn. They were going to crash!

"Watch out!" shouted Wilson. "Chugger down!"

Koko heard Emery coming down the track and heard Wilson's cry for help. She knew Wilson was really in trouble. "Hold tight, Wilson!" shouted Koko. She raced back and pulled Wilson out of the way.

"Thanks," said Wilson. "But pulling me is going to make you lose the race."

"Making sure you're safe is way more important than winning," said Koko.

Koko towed Wilson all the way to the end of the race. They were just in time to see Old Puffer Pete cross the finish line.

"And the winner is . . . Old Puffer Pete!" shouted Vee.

"I'm sorry for tricking you, Koko. If you hadn't stopped to help me, you still could have won," said Wilson.

"I'm sorry I was so silly about wanting to win," said Koko.

"Friends?" asked Wilson.

"Friends!" Koko agreed.

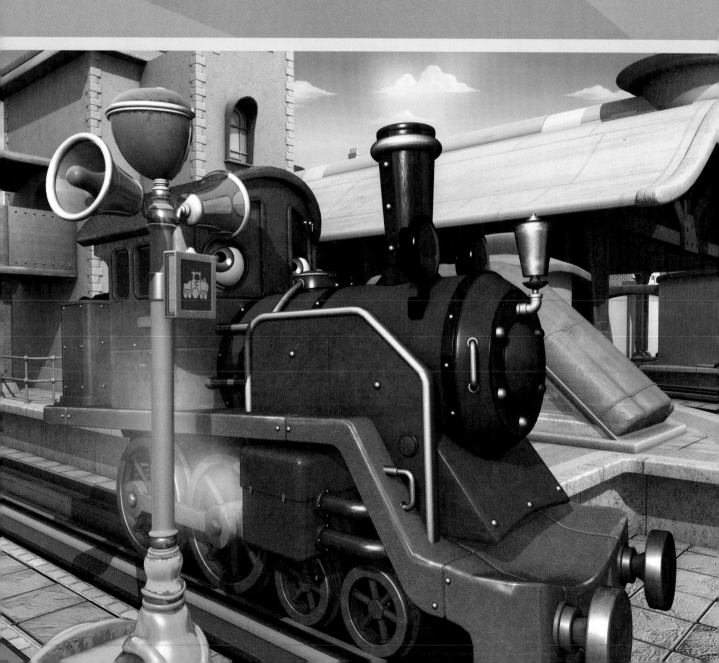

"Vee, I think someone else should have the trophy," Pete said. "I didn't race from the beginning."

"Well . . ." Vee replied. "I do know a chugger who didn't come in first. But she gave up her lead to help a friend. That makes her a true champion. I say this year's champion is . . . Koko!"

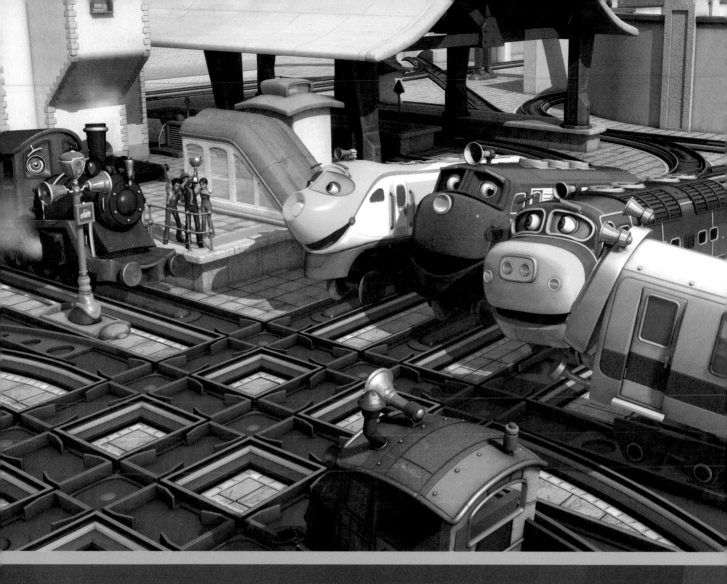

"Hooray for Koko!"

All the trains cheered for the new Chugger Champion!